Little Mermaids and Ugly Ducklings

Favorite Fairy Tales *by*
Hans Christian Andersen

Little
Mermaids
and Ugly
Ducklings

illustrated by
Gennady Spirin

chronicle books · san francisco

To Hans Christian Andersen — G. S.

Text © 2001 by Ivy Pages.
Illustrations © 2001 by Gennady Spirin.
All rights reserved.

Book design by Bea Jackson, Ivy Pages.
Typeset in Cochin.
Text edited by Susan Pearson.
The illustrations in this book were rendered in watercolor and colored pencil.

Printed in China.

Library of Congress Cataloging-in-Publication Data
Andersen, H. C. (Hans Christian), 1805-1875.
Little mermaids and ugly ducklings: favorite fairy tales/by Hans Christian Andersen;
illustrated by Gennady Spirin.
p. cm.
ISBN 0-8118-1954-X
1. Fairy tales—Denmark. 2. Children's stories,
Danish—Translations into English. [1. Fairy tales. 2. Short stories.]   I. Spirin, Gennady, ill. II. Title.
PZ8.A54 Ug 2001
839.8'136--dc21
[[Fi
2001000202
Distributed in Canada by Raincoast Books
9050 Shaughnessy Street, Vancouver, British Columbia V6P 6E5

10 9 8 7 6 5 4 3 2 1

Chronicle Books LLC
85 Second Street, San Francisco, California 94105

www.chroniclebooks.com/Kids

Contents

Foreword

Hans Christian Andersen was born near Copenhagen, Denmark, in the early 1800s. As a young man, he struggled to find his artistic voice, first through acting, then playwriting, then novels, and finally through fairy tales. With his fairy tales Andersen created a new style of literature. Even today, his stories remain refreshing and new. They speak directly and intimately to his readers. They are also a fantastic journey, taking us to distant lands both real and imagined.

Andersen loved to travel, and he was inspired by folk legends he collected on his journeys throughout Europe and Asia Minor. Remarkably, however, while he shows us the differences in cultures around the world, through his stories he also shows us the universality of human spirit. And sometimes he carries us to places that are no farther than our own backyards, but shows us life from a point of view that we may not have considered before.

His characters, from the little mermaid to the ugly duckling to the emperor of China, learn universal life lessons from their experiences, lessons that are still vital to the way we live today. From Andersen, we learn to trust in ourselves, to believe that beauty is more than skin deep, to realize that the gifts we find in nature are precious, and that the sacrifices we make for love are at the heart and soul of who we are as humans.

This collection, drawn from some of the earliest translations of his work, from his native Danish into English, and lavishly illustrated by artist Gennady Spirin, gathers some of Hans Christian Andersen's most popular tales. Read and loved by generations, these stories have remained astonishingly alive and fresh for more than 150 years. It is remarkable that so much of the world around us has changed from Andersen's time, and yet so much of what lives in our hearts remains the same.

The Ugly Duckling

It was beautiful in the country, for it was summertime. The cornfields were yellow, the oats were green, the hay was stacked in the meadows, and the stork strutted about on his long red legs and chattered in Egyptian, for this was the language he had learned from his mother. The fields and meadows were surrounded by great forests, and in the midst of the forests there were deep lakes.

In the midst of the sunshine lay an old farm surrounded by deep canals. From the stone wall of the farmhouse down to the water's edge, the plants grew so tall that children could stand upright under them. It was just as wild as the deepest woods, and here sat a duck on her nest. She had nearly hatched her little ducklings, but she was quite tired of sitting, for it had taken her a long time, and she seldom received any visitors. The other ducks liked swimming about in the canals better than waddling up to sit under the leaves and gossip with her.

At last one egg after another began to crack. "Peep-peep!" cried the little ducklings as they popped their heads out.

"Quack-quack!" said the mother duck, and the little ones tumbled out of their eggs just as fast as they could, peering all about them under the green leaves. Their mother let the ducklings look as much as they pleased, for green is good for the eyes.

"How large the world is!" said the ducklings, for they had much more room now than when they had been inside their eggshells.

"Do you imagine that this is the whole world?" said their mother. "No, indeed. The world stretches far away, all the way to the other side of the garden and into the parson's field, though I have never been there myself. I suppose you are all here now?" She got up and looked about. "No, not yet! The biggest egg still remains. How long is this going to take?" she said as she settled herself back on the nest.

"Well, how are you getting on?" asked an old duck who came to pay her a visit.

"This egg is taking such a long time," said the sitting duck. "It will not crack. But look at all the others. They are the finest ducklings I have ever seen."

"Let me see the egg that won't crack," said the old duck. "It may be a turkey's egg. I was fooled like that once, and I had no end of trouble with the creatures, for they

were all afraid of the water. I simply could not get them into it. Let me see that egg! Yes, it's a turkey's egg, all right. You just leave it alone and teach the other children how to swim."

"I will sit on it a little longer," said the duck. "I have sat so long already, I may as well sit a few days more."

"Well, suit yourself," said the old duck, and off she waddled.

At last the big egg cracked. "Peep-peep!" said the young duckling, and out he popped. The mother duck stared at him. How big and ugly he was!

"None of the others look like this!" she said. "Could he really be a turkey chick? Well, we shall soon see. Into the water he shall go, even if I have to push him in myself."

The next day was bright and beautiful, and the mother duck took her whole family down to the canal. Splash!—into the water she jumped. "Quack-quack!" she said, and one after another the ducklings tumbled in. The water closed over their heads for an instant, but they bobbed right back up and swam beautifully, their legs seeming to know on their own what to do. So there they were, all of them swimming about in the water, even the big ugly gray one.

"No, this cannot be a turkey," said the mother duck. "See how beautifully he uses his legs, how gracefully he carries himself. He is my own child after all. In fact, he's rather handsome when you look at him properly. Quack-quack! Now come along, children, and I will take you out into the world and introduce you to the poultry yard. But stay close to me all the time so that no one steps on you—and look out for the cat!"

And so they came into the poultry yard, where a fearful to-do was going on. Two ducks were fighting over an eel's head—but in the end, the cat got it.

"That's how things go in this world," said the mother duck with a sigh, for she would have liked to have the eel's head, too. "Now step lively. Let me see you looking smart. And bend your necks to the old duck over there. She is an aristocrat. She has Spanish blood in her veins, and that accounts for her size. Now don't turn your toes in. A well-brought-up duckling walks with legs wide apart, just like mother. That's it. Now bend your necks and say quack!"

And so they did. But the other ducks looked at them and said quite loudly, "Well, now we're going to have this new lot, too—as if there weren't enough of us already. And just look at that big ugly duckling! We won't stand having him around!" And one duck flew up and bit him on the neck.

"Leave him alone," said his mother. "He is doing no harm to anyone."

"Maybe not," said the biter, "but he is so big and ugly, he deserves to be bitten."

"Your children are very pretty, mother," said the old duck. "Except for that one. He is a failure. I wish you could make him over."

"That cannot be done, Your Highness," said the mother duck. "He may not be pretty, but he is very good tempered, and he swims beautifully, quite as well as any of the others— indeed, I may even say better. I daresay he will grow handsome in time. He has been lying too long in the egg—that is why his shape is not quite right." She scratched the duckling's neck and patted his head. I believe he will be very strong, and he will get along very well."

"Well, it seems your other ducklings are pretty enough," said the old duck. "Make yourself at home, and if you find an eel's head, you may bring it to me."

After that they all felt quite at home—all except for the duckling that came out of the last egg and looked so ugly. He was bitten and pushed about and sneered at by both the ducks and the hens. "He is too big," they all said, and the turkey-cock, who was born with spurs and so thought himself an emperor, puffed himself out like a ship in full sail, strutted straight up to the ugly duckling, and gobbled until he was red in the face. The poor duckling didn't know what to do. He was in despair because he was so ugly and the whole poultry yard hated him.

As the days passed, it got worse and worse. The poor little duckling was chased by everyone. Even his own brothers and sisters were mean to him. "If only the cat would take you, you ugly thing!" they would say. The ducks bit him, the hens pecked him, and the girl who fed the poultry kicked him.

At last the ugly duckling ran away, right over the hedge, where the little birds in the bushes flew up in alarm.

"It's because I'm so ugly," thought the duckling, and he ran on until he came to the great marsh where the wild ducks lived. There, tired and miserable, he spent the night.

In the morning, the wild ducks flew over to inspect their new companion. "Where do you come from?" they asked. "You are uncommonly ugly, but that is all the same to us, so long as you don't marry into our family."

The poor duckling had never thought of getting married! All he ever wanted was to be allowed to lie in the rushes and drink a little of the marsh water.

He stayed there two whole days. Then two wild geese—or rather wild ganders—came by. They had not been long out of the egg, which is why they were so rude.

"You're so ugly that we've taken a fancy to you," they said. "Would you like to join us? There's another marsh not far from here. There are some charming wild geese there, all unmarried, and they can all say quack. They'd find you very interesting, you're so ugly."

Suddenly two loud BANGs sounded in the air and the two ganders fell dead in the reeds. BANG! BANG! went the guns again, and whole flocks of wild geese flew up from the reeds, while more shots rang out. It was a large shooting party and the hunters were all around the marsh, some of them lying in the reeds, others sitting on tree branches over the rushes. Blue gun-smoke rose in clouds through the dark trees and floated away across the water.

Then the hunting dogs came splashing through the shallow water. The poor duckling hid his head under his wing in fear, but just at that moment a huge dog appeared right beside him. His tongue hung out of his mouth and his eyes glared wickedly. He thrust his nose close to the duckling and bared his sharp teeth, but then, splash!—away he went without touching a feather.

"Thank heaven!" sighed the duckling. "I am so ugly that even the dog won't bite me!" Then he lay still while the shots whizzed among the reeds as the hunters fired again and again.

Late in the day the shooting stopped, but even then the poor duckling did not dare move. He waited several more hours before he began to look around. Then he hurried away from the marsh as fast as he could. Over the meadows and through the fields he ran. It was hard work, for the wind was strong, but toward evening he reached a poor cottage. It was so run-down that it remained standing only because it could not make up its mind which way to fall.

The wind was blowing so hard that the duckling had to sit down so as not to be blown away, and it was getting worse and worse. Then he noticed that the door of the cottage had come off one of its hinges and was hanging crookedly, so that he could slip through the crack into the room. And he did.

Here lived an old woman with her cat and her hen. The cat, whom she called Sonny, could arch his back and purr and even give off sparks, but only when you stroked him the wrong way. The hen had stumpy little legs, and so was called Chickabiddy Shortshanks. She laid plenty of eggs, and the old woman loved her as if she were her own child. In the morning they immediately discovered the strange duckling, and the cat began to purr and the hen to cackle.

"What is the matter?" said the old woman, peering around. But she could not see well, and she thought that the duckling was a fat duck who'd gotten lost. "A capital find!" she thought.

"Now I shall have duck eggs—if only this is not a drake. We will have to find out." So the duckling was put on a trial for three weeks, but of course no eggs came.

The cat was master of the house and the hen was mistress, and they were always talking as if they were half the world, and the better half at that. The duckling thought that others might have a different opinion, but the hen would not hear of it.

"Can you lay eggs?" she asked. "No? Well, then, hold your tongue."

And the cat said, "Can you arch your back, or purr, or give off sparks? No? Then you have no right to an opinion when sensible people are talking."

The duckling sat in a corner saying nothing. Then he began to think of fresh air and sunshine, and he was filled with such a powerful longing to float on the water that he could not help telling the hen about it.

"What is the matter with you?" she said. "You have nothing to do. That is why you get such nonsense into your head. Lay an egg or purr and you will get over it."

"But it is so lovely to swim," said the duckling, "so delicious to feel the water close over your head when you dive down to the bottom!"

"A real pleasure that must be!" said the hen. "You are certainly going mad! Just ask the cat, who is the wisest person I know, if he likes to float on water or dive beneath it. Or ask our mistress—there is not a wiser old woman in the world. Do you think that she would like to float on water or feel it closing over her head?"

"You don't understand me," said the duckling.

"Well, if we don't understand you, then who will?" said the hen. "You surely don't mean to say that you are wiser than the cat and the old woman, not to mention me? Here you are in a warm room with good company who can teach you something. You should thank the stars for your good fortune. But instead you chatter on and are most disagreeable!

"I only speak these unpleasant truths for your own good—what else are friends for? Now get on with laying eggs and learning to purr!"

"I think I will go out again into the wide world," said the duckling.

"Then by all means, do that!" said the hen.

So the duckling went. He swam in the water and dived, but he was shunned by every other creature because he was so ugly.

Soon autumn came. The leaves in the forest turned yellow and brown, and the wind took hold of them and sent them dancing. The sky looked cold, and the clouds were heavy with hail and snow. And on the stone wall, a raven stood shivering and screeching "Caw! Caw!" It was enough to make anyone shiver, and the poor duckling was quite miserable.

One evening as the sun was setting, a flock of large birds rose out of the bushes. Their white feathers were dazzling and they had long, slender necks. The duckling had never seen anything so beautiful. They were swans, and they uttered wondrous cries as they spread their magnificent wings and flew toward warmer climes. Higher and higher they rose, and the ugly duckling felt a strange sensation as he watched them. He circled round and round in the water like a wheel, craning his neck after them, then uttered a cry so piercing and strange that he frightened himself. When he could no longer see them, he dived right to the bottom, so that when he came up again he was nearly out of breath. He did not know what the birds were called or where they were flying, but he loved them as he had never loved anything else. He was not at all envious of them, for he never thought that he could wish for such beauty for himself. He would have been happy if they would simply put up with his company, poor ugly thing that he was.

Winter came and the days grew colder and colder. The duckling had to swim about in the water to keep it from freezing, and every night the hole in which he was swimming grew smaller. Soon the duckling had to keep paddling all the time so that the water wouldn't freeze right around him. At last he was worn out and had to stop, and before long he was frozen fast in the ice.

Early in the morning a farmer came along and saw him, knocked a hole in the ice with his wooden shoe, and carried the duckling home to his wife. There he soon revived.

The farmer's children wanted to play with him, but the duckling thought they would hurt him, and in his fright he flew into the milk can and the milk splashed all over the floor. The farmer's wife screamed and threw up her hands. The duckling flew into the butter tub, and then into the flour barrel and out again. What a mess he looked! The farmer's wife shrieked and tried to hit him with the fire tongs, and the children tumbled over each other trying to catch him and shouting with laughter. Luckily the door was open, and out he rushed through the new fallen snow and into the bushes, where he lay exhausted.

It would be far too sad to tell of all the misery the duckling had to endure throughout that hard winter. But at last one day, as he was lying in the marsh among the reeds, the sun began to shine warmly again. Larks began to sing. Spring had come!

All at once the duckling lifted his wings. They flapped with much greater strength than they had before and bore him easily aloft. He was flying! Before he knew it, he came to a large garden where apple trees were in full blossom, and the air smelled sweetly of lilacs bending over the river. Just in front of him, out of a thicket came three beautiful white swans, ruffling their feathers as they floated lightly on the water. The duckling recognized the magnificent creatures and was overcome by a strange feeling of sadness.

"I will fly over to them, those royal birds, and they will kill me, because I, who am so ugly, dare to approach them. But it will be better to be killed by them than to be bitten by the ducks, pecked by the chickens, and kicked by the maid who looks after the poultry yard, and to suffer another hard winter. So he flew into the water and swam toward the beautiful swans. They saw him, ruffled their feathers, and swam to meet him.

The poor creature bowed his head toward the water and awaited his death. But what did he see reflected in the clear water? He saw his own image—but he was no longer a clumsy, dark gray bird, ugly and hateful to look at. He was—a swan! The young swan suddenly felt quite glad for all the misery he had suffered, for he could truly appreciate the happiness that swelled in him now. The large swans swam around him and stroked him with their beaks.

Some little children came into the garden then with bread and corn, which they began to throw into the water. "There is a new one!" the smallest of them shouted. "Yes, a new one has arrived!" the other children cried out in delight, and they clapped their hands and danced around their father and mother. "The new one is the prettiest," they all agreed. "He is so young and so lovely."

The old swans bowed to him. This made him feel shy, and he hid his head under his wing. He did not know quite what to think. He was so very happy, but he did not feel proud at all, for a good heart never becomes proud. He thought of how he had been persecuted and despised, and now he heard them all saying that he was the most beautiful of all the birds. It makes no difference if you hatch in a duck's nest when you come from a swan's egg.

The lilac bush bowed down its branches to him, and the sun shone warm and bright. Then he rustled his feathers, curved his slender neck, and cried joyfully from the depths of his heart: "I never dreamed of so much happiness when I was the Ugly Duckling!" &

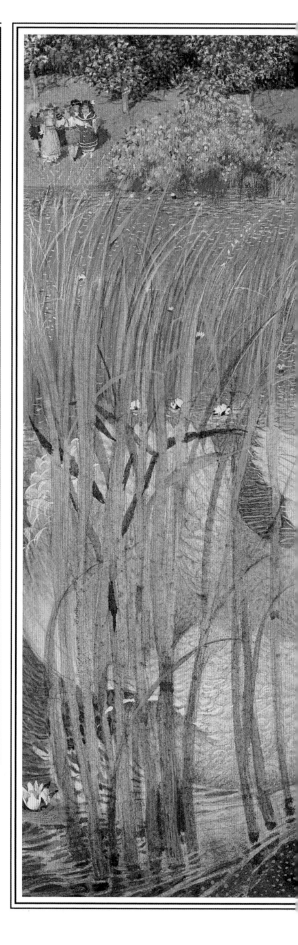

Thumbelina

There once was a woman who wished very much to have a little child, but as she had no idea where to find one, she went at last to a witch and said, "I should so very much like to have a little child of my own. Can you tell me where I might find one?"

"Oh, that can be easily managed," said the witch. "Here is a barleycorn. It is far different from those that grow in farmers' fields. Put it into a flower pot and see what will happen."

"Thank you," said the woman, and she gave the witch twelve shillings, which was the price of the barleycorn. Then she went home and planted it.

Immediately there grew from it a large handsome flower like a tulip, but with its petals tightly closed. "What a beautiful flower!" said the woman, and she kissed the red and gold petals. As she did so, the flower opened. Within it, seated on the green velvet stamens, was a very delicate and graceful little maiden. She was scarcely half as long as a thumb, and so the woman called her Thumbelina.

A walnut shell, elegantly polished, served her for a cradle. She lay on a mattress of blue-violet leaves with a rose petal for a cover. Here she slept at night, but during the day she played on a table where the woman had placed a plate full of water. Around this plate were wreaths of flowers with their stems in the water, upon which floated a large tulip leaf which served Thumbelina for a boat. Here the little maiden sat and rowed herself from side to side with two white horsehairs for oars—a very pretty sight indeed! As she played, Thumbelina often sang, and her voice was so sweet and delicate that nothing so beautiful had ever been heard before.

One night while she lay in her pretty bed, a large, ugly, wet toad hopped up on the table. "What a pretty little wife this would make for my son!" said the toad, and she seized the walnut shell in which Thumbelina lay sleeping and jumped out through the window into the garden.

The toad lived with her son on the muddy bank of a broad stream in the garden. The son was even uglier than his mother, and when he saw the pretty little maiden in her elegant bed he could only cry, "Croak, croak, croak! Brek-ke-ke-kex!"

"Don't speak so loudly or she will wake," said the mother toad, "and then she might run away, for she is as light as swan's down. We will put her on one of the water-lily leaves out in the stream. It will be like an island to her, she is so light and small, and she will not be able to escape. Then we will hurry to prepare a lovely room under the mud where you two will live after you are married."

Far out in the stream grew a number of water lilies with broad green leaves that floated on top of the water. The old toad swam with the walnut shell, out to the largest leaf, and there she left Thumbelina, asleep in her little bed.

The little maiden woke very early in the morning. When she discovered where she was, she began to cry, for she could see nothing but water on every side of the large green leaf and no way of reaching the land.

Meanwhile, the old toad had been busy under the mud, decking the bridal room with rushes and yellow wildflowers to make it look pretty for her new daughter-in-law. Then she swam out with her ugly son to the leaf on which she had placed poor Thumbelina. She wanted to fetch the pretty little bed and put it in the bridal chamber to make everything ready for her.

The old toad bowed low in the water to Thumbelina and said, "Here is my son. He will be your husband, and you will live happily together in the mud by the stream."

"Croak, croak, croak! Brek-ke-ke-kex!" was all her son could say for himself.

So the toads took the elegant little bed and swam away with it, leaving Thumbelina all alone on the green leaf. She sat and wept, for she could not bear to think of living with the old toad and having her ugly son for a husband.

The little fishes who swam about in the water beneath had seen the toad and heard what she said, so they lifted their heads above the water to have a look at the little maiden. As soon as they caught sight of her, they saw how very pretty she was, and it made them sorry to think that she must go and live with the ugly toads. No, that must never be! So they gathered around the green stalk that held the leaf on which the little maiden stood, and gnawed it in two. The leaf floated down the stream, carrying Thumbelina far away, where the horrible toads could not find her.

Thumbelina sailed on. The little birds in the bushes watched her and sang, "What a lovely little creature!" The leaf floated farther and farther, until it brought her to another land. Now the toads could not possibly reach her, and the country through which she sailed was beautiful. The sun shone upon the water until it glittered like liquid gold. A graceful little butterfly fluttered around her and at last alighted on the leaf, for it liked Thumbelina. Thumbelina was delighted. She took off her ribbon, tied one end of it around the butterfly, and fastened the other end to the leaf. With the butterfly to pull her, she could sail faster than ever.

Just then a large beetle came flying along. The moment he caught sight of Thumbelina he clasped his pinchers around her delicate waist and flew up into a tree. The green leaf floated away down the stream, and the butterfly flew with it, for he was fastened to the leaf and could not get away.

Oh, how frightened poor Thumbelina was when the beetle flew off with her into the tree! And how sorry she felt for the beautiful white butterfly she had tied to the leaf. But the beetle did not care at all about that. He sat beside her on a large green leaf, gave her honey from the flowers to eat, and told her she was very pretty, though not at all like a beetle.

Before long, all the beetles that lived in the tree came to look at Thumbelina. The young lady beetles stared closely at her. "She has only two legs!" said one. "How ugly that looks!"

"She has no feelers!" cried another. "And such a thin waist! Why, she's as ugly as a human being!"

The beetle who had carried her away had thought her quite pretty at first, but when all the others called her ugly he felt that they must be right and wanted nothing more to do with her. So he flew down from the tree and set her on a daisy. Thumbelina wept to think she was so ugly that even the beetles would not have her. And yet she was really the loveliest little creature anyone could imagine, as fine and delicate as a rose leaf.

All summer long poor Thumbelina lived alone in the great forest. She wove herself a bed of grass and hung it under a broad leaf that sheltered her from the rain. She sucked honey from the flowers for food, and drank dew from the leaves every morning. So the summer passed away, and the autumn, and then came winter—the long, cold winter. All the birds who had sung to her so sweetly flew away, and the trees and flowers withered. The large leaf under which she had lived shriveled into nothing but a dry yellow stalk. Poor Thumbelina was terribly cold, for her clothes were in rags, and she was so delicate that she nearly froze to death.

When it began to snow, each snowflake that fell on her was like a whole shovelful falling on one of us, for we are tall, but she was only an inch high. She wrapped herself in a dry leaf, but it cracked apart and could not keep her warm, and she shivered with the cold.

Near the forest lay a large cornfield in which the corn had long since been cut. As she made her way through the dry stubble that stood on the frozen ground, it seemed to her as if she were struggling through a great wood. Oh how she trembled with the cold! At last she came to a doorway. A field mouse had a little den under the corn stubble, where she dwelt in warmth and comfort with a whole roomful of corn, a kitchen, and a beautiful dining room. Poor Thumbelina stood at the door, just like a beggar girl, and asked for a small piece of barleycorn, for she hadn't had a morsel to eat for two days.

"You poor little creature," said the field mouse, who was really a good old field mouse. "Come into my warm room and dine with me. You are quite welcome to stay with me all winter if you like, but you must keep my rooms clean and neat and tell me stories, for I am very fond of them." And Thumbelina did all that the field mouse asked, and lived very comfortably.

"We shall have a visitor soon," said the field mouse one day. "My neighbor pays me a visit once a week. He is better off than I am. He has large rooms and wears a beautiful black velvet coat. If you could only have him for a husband, you would be well provided for indeed! But he is blind, so you must tell him some of your prettiest stories."

Thumbelina did not feel at all interested in this neighbor, for he was a mole. However, he came and paid his visit, dressed in his black velvet coat.

"He is very rich and learned, and his house is twenty times larger than mine," said the field mouse.

The mole was rich and learned, no doubt, but he said he did not like the sun and the pretty flowers, though the truth was he had never seen them. Thumbelina had to sing "Lady Bird, Lady Bird, Fly Away Home" and other pretty songs to him, and the mole fell in love with her because she had such a sweet voice, but he said nothing yet, for he was very cautious.

A short time before, the mole had dug a long passage under the earth that led from his house to the fieldmouse's. Here the field mouse had permission to walk with Thumbelina whenever she liked. But he warned them not to be alarmed at the sight of a dead bird that lay in the passage. It must have died only recently and been buried just where the mole had dug his tunnel.

The mole took a piece of touchwood that glowed in the dark and lit their way through the long passageway. When they came to the spot where the bird lay, he pushed his broad nose through the ceiling. The earth gave way so that there was a large hole, and daylight shone into the tunnel.

There lay the dead swallow, his beautiful wings folded close to his sides, his feet and head drawn up under his feathers. The poor bird must have died of the cold. It made Thumbelina very sad, for she loved the little birds that had sung for her so beautifully all summer long. But the mole just pushed the bird aside with his crooked legs and said, "He will sing no more now. How miserable it must be to be born a little bird! I am thankful that none of my children will ever be birds, for they can do nothing but cry 'Tweet-tweet!' and they always die of hunger in the winter."

"Yes, you may well say so, you clever mole!" exclaimed the field mouse. "What is the point of his singing, if when winter comes he must either starve or freeze to death?"

Thumbelina said nothing, but when the other two had turned their backs on the bird, she knelt down and stroked the soft feathers that covered his head and kissed his closed eyelids. "Perhaps you were one of the lovely birds who sang to me so sweetly this summer," she said. "How much pleasure you gave me, you dear pretty bird."

The mole now closed up the hole through which the daylight shone, then saw the ladies home. But during the night Thumbelina could not sleep. She got out of bed and wove a large, beautiful carpet of hay. Then she carried it down to the dead bird and spread it over him. Around him she spread petals from flowers she had found in the field mouse's room. It was as soft as wool and would warm him as he lay in the cold earth.

"Farewell, you pretty little bird," she said. "Farewell! Thank you for your beautiful song last summer, when all the trees were green and the warm sun shone down on us." And she lay her head on the bird's breast.

Suddenly it seemed as if something inside the bird went thump! thump! It was the bird's heart! He was not really dead, only stunned and numb with the cold. The warmth had restored him to life. Thumbelina trembled with fright, for the bird was a great deal larger than herself. But, taking courage, she spread the petals more thickly over the poor swallow. Then she took the leaf she used for her own coverlet and laid it over his head.

The next night she again stole out to see him. He was alive but very weak, and could only open his eyes for a moment to look at Thumbelina, who held a piece of glowing touchwood in her hand, for she had no other lantern.

"Thank you, pretty little maiden," said the sick swallow. "I have been so well warmed that I shall soon regain my strength and be able to fly out again into the warm sunshine."

"Oh, it is so cold out now!" she said. "It is snowing and freezing. Stay in your warm bed and I will take care of you."

Thumbelina brought the swallow some water in a flower petal, and after he drank he told her that he had wounded one of his wings on a thornbush and could not fly as fast as the other swallows, who were soon far away on their journey to warm countries. At last he had fallen to the ground. He could remember no more and did not know how he came to be here, where she had found him.

The swallow remained underground that whole winter, and Thumbelina nursed him with tenderness and love. She told the mole and the field mouse nothing about it, for they did not like swallows.

At last spring came and the sun warmed the earth. Then the swallow bade farewell to Thumbelina, and she opened the hole in the ceiling that the mole had made, and the sun shone in on them. The swallow asked if she would like to go with him. She could sit on his back, he said, and he would fly away with her into the green woods. But Thumbelina knew how much the field mouse would grieve if she left in that manner.

"No," she said. "I cannot."

"Farewell, then, you dear, good little maiden," said the swallow. And he flew out into the sunshine.

Thumbelina looked after him and tears filled her eyes, she was so fond of the swallow.

"Tweet-tweet," he sang as he flew into the green woods.

How sad Thumbelina was now. She was never allowed to go out into the warm sunshine. The corn that had been sown in the field above the mouse's home grew so high that it was like a giant forest to Thumbelina.

One day the field mouse announced, "You are going to be married, Thumbelina. My neighbor the mole has asked for you. What good fortune for a poor child like you! Now we must prepare your wedding clothes. They will be both woolen and linen. You must lack nothing when you become the mole's wife."

Thumbelina had to turn the spindle while four spiders, hired by the field mouse, wove both day and night. Every evening the mole visited her. He was always talking of the time when summer would be over and he would wed Thumbelina. Now, he said, the heat of the sun was so great that it burned the earth hard as stone.

Thumbelina was not happy, for she did not like the tiresome mole. Every morning when the sun rose, and every evening when it went down, she crept to the door, and as the wind blew aside the ears of corn so that she could see the blue sky, she thought how beautiful and bright it seemed out there, and wished so much to see her dear swallow again. But he did not return, for by this time he had flown far away into the lovely green forest.

When autumn came, Thumbelina's outfit was ready. "In four weeks the wedding will take place," said the field mouse. But Thumbelina wept and said she would not marry the disagreeable mole.

"Nonsense!" replied the field mouse. "Don't be obstinate or I shall bite you with my teeth! He is a very handsome mole. The queen herself does not wear more beautiful velvet and furs. His kitchens and cellars are full. You ought to be thankful for such good fortune."

So the wedding day came, and the mole was to take Thumbelina to live with him deep under the earth, never again to see the warm sun, because he did not like it. The poor child was very unhappy at the thought of saying farewell to the beautiful sun, and, as the field mouse had given her permission to stand at the door, she went to look at it once more.

"Farewell, bright sun!" she cried, stretching out her arms to it. Then she walked a short distance from the house, for the corn had been cut, and only the dry stubble remained in the fields. "Farewell, farewell," she repeated, wrapping her arms around a little red flower growing just by her side. "Greet the little swallow for me if you should see him again."

Suddenly a voice just above Thumbelina's head sang, "Tweet-tweet!" She looked up, and there was the swallow, flying close by. When he spied Thumbelina he was delighted. She told him how she dreaded having to marry the ugly mole and live forever after beneath the earth, never to see the bright sun again. And as she told him, she wept.

"Cold winter is coming," said the swallow, "and I am going to fly away to warmer countries. Will you go with me? You can sit on my back and fasten yourself on with your sash. We can fly away from the ugly mole and his gloomy rooms—far, far away over the mountains, into warmer lands where the sun shines more brightly than here, where it is always summer and lovely flowers always bloom. Fly with me now, dear little Thumbelina, you who saved my life when I lay frozen in that dark, dreary passage."

"Yes! I will go with you!" said Thumbelina. And she seated herself on his back, and tied her sash to the root of one of his strongest feathers.

The swallow rose into the air and flew over the forest and over the sea, high above the highest mountains, covered with eternal snow. To keep from freezing, Thumbelina crept under the bird's warm feathers, keeping her tiny head uncovered so that she might admire the beautiful lands over which they passed.

At length they arrived in the warm countries where the sun shines brightly all year. Here, on the hedges and by the wayside, grew purple, green, and white grapes. Lemons and oranges hung from trees in the woods, and the air was fragrant with myrtles and orange blossoms. Beautiful children ran along the country lanes, playing with large bright butterflies, and as the swallow flew farther and farther, every place appeared still more lovely.

At last they came to a blue lake. By the side of it, shaded by trees of the deepest green, stood an ancient palace of dazzling white marble. Vines clustered around its lofty pillars,

and at the top were many swallows' nests. One of these was the home of the swallow who had brought Thumbelina to this land.

"That is my house," said the swallow, "but you would not be comfortable living there. Choose for yourself one of the pretty flowers growing below, and I will set you down on it. Then you shall have everything you can wish to make you happy."

"How lovely!" Thumbelina cried, clapping her little hands for joy.

On the ground lay a large marble pillar which, in falling, had broken into three pieces. Between these pieces grew the most beautiful white flowers, and the swallow flew down with Thumbelina and placed her on one of the broad petals. How surprised she was to see, in the middle of the flower, a tiny man! He had a gold crown on his head and delicate wings on his shoulders and was not much bigger than Thumbelina herself. A tiny man and a tiny woman dwell in every flower, and this was the king of them all.

"How beautiful he is!" whispered Thumbelina to the swallow.

The little king was at first quite frightened by the bird, who was a giant compared to such a delicate creature as himself. But when he saw Thumbelina he was delighted. He thought her the loveliest little maiden he had ever seen. He took the gold crown from his head and placed it on hers; he asked her name and if she would be his wife and the queen of all the flowers.

Now this was truly a very different sort of husband from the toad's son or the mole with his black velvet fur! And Thumbelina said yes to the handsome little king.

Then all the flowers opened, and out of them came tiny men and women so dainty that they were a delight to behold. Each of them brought Thumbelina a present, and the most wonderful of all was a pair of beautiful wings. They fastened the wings to Thumbelina's shoulders so that she could fly from flower to flower.

There was much rejoicing, and the swallow, who sat above them in his nest, was asked to sing a wedding song, which he did as well as he could, though in his heart he was rather sad, for he was very fond of Thumbelina and would have liked never to part from her again.

"You should no longer be called Thumbelina," said the little king of the flowers. "It is an ugly name, and you are so very beautiful. We will call you Maia."

"Farewell, farewell," said the swallow as he set out the next spring to fly back to Denmark, where he had a nest over the window of a certain house in which lives the man who writes fairy tales. The swallow sang, "Tweet-tweet," and from his song came the whole story.

19

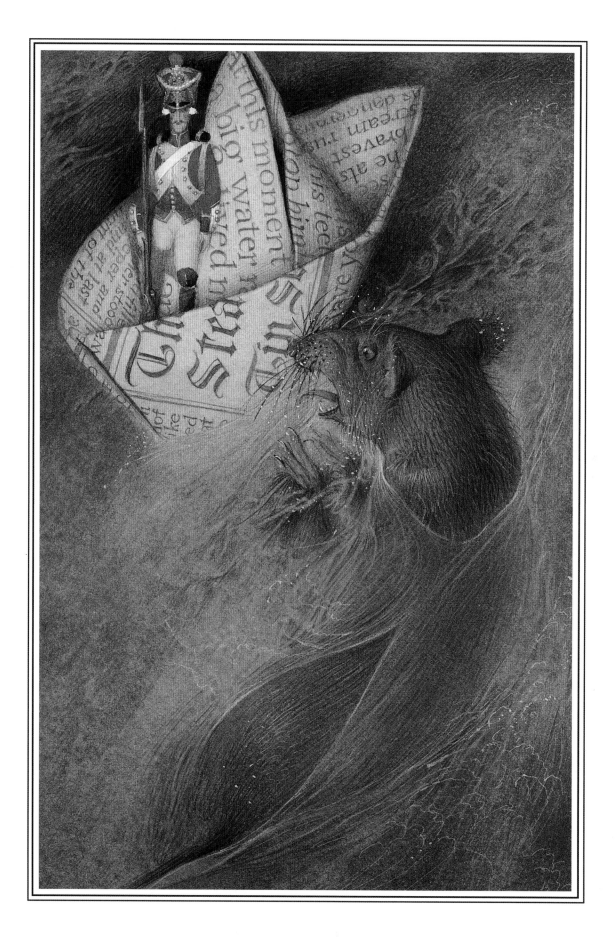

The Steadfast Tin Soldier

There were once twenty-five tin soldiers who were all brothers, for they had all been made from the same old tin spoon. They carried their muskets on their shoulders and stood at attention, looking straight in front of them. Their uniforms were red and blue, and very handsome indeed.

The very first thing they heard in this world, when the lid was taken off their box, was the words, "Tin soldiers!" shouted by a little boy, clapping his hands. The soldiers had been given to him because it was his birthday, and now he set them up on the table.

All the soldiers were just alike except for one, who had only one leg. He was the last to be cast, and there had not been enough tin. Yet he stood just as steadily on his one leg as the others on their two, and it was he who became famous.

There were a number of other toys on the table with the tin soldiers, but the most splendid was a beautiful castle made of cardboard. Through its small windows you could see straight into the rooms. Outside, little trees stood around a small mirror, which was meant to look like a lake. Wax swans swam on it and were reflected in the mirror. All this was very pretty—but prettiest of all was a little maid who stood at the open door of the castle. She was also cut out of cardboard, but she had a skirt of the finest gauze and wore a narrow blue ribbon over her shoulder like a sash, in the middle of which was a sparkling sequin almost as big as her whole face. The little maid stretched out both her arms, for she was a dancer, and lifted one of her legs so high that the tin soldier could not see it at all, and thought that she had only one leg, like himself.

"There is just the wife for me!" the tin soldier thought. "But she is very grand and lives in a castle. I have only a box, and all twenty-five of us must share it. That is no place for her. But I would like to make her acquaintance, all the same." So he hid behind a snuffbox on the table, where he could easily watch the charming little maid, who continued to stand on one leg without losing her balance.

That evening all the other tin soldiers were put back into the box, and the people in the house went to bed. Then the toys began to play: they paid visits, they went to war, they gave balls. The tin soldiers rattled in their box, for they wanted to join in the fun, but they could not get the lid off. The nutcrackers were turning somersaults, the slate pencil danced on the slate, and there was so much noise that the canary woke up and began to talk in verse. The only two who did not move from their places were the tin soldier and the little dancer. She continued to stand on the tips of her toes with both her arms outstretched, and the tin soldier stood just as firmly on his one leg and did not take his eyes off her, even for a moment.

Then the clock struck twelve, and snap! up flew the lid of the snuffbox. But there was no snuff inside. No! There was a tiny goblin!

"Tin soldier," cried the goblin, "keep your eyes to yourself!" But the tin soldier pretended not to hear.

"All right, then," said the goblin. "Just you wait till tomorrow!"

When the children got up in the morning, the tin soldier was put in the window, and whether it was the goblin or the draft that did it, all of a sudden the window flew open and the soldier fell out, head over heels, from the third floor. It was a terrible fall. He landed on his helmet with his only leg straight up in the air and his bayonet stuck between the paving stones. The little boy and a servant went down at once to find him, but although they nearly stepped on him, they could not see him. If only the little tin soldier had cried, "Here I am!" he might have been rescued, but he did not think it proper to shout when he was in uniform.

Then it began to rain, and the little boy and the servant went back inside. The rain fell faster and faster until it became a real downpour. When it was over, two street boys came along.

"Look!" said one of them. "Here's a tin soldier. Let's send him to sea."

So they made a little boat from a newspaper, put the tin soldier in it, and sent him sailing down the gutter while they ran alongside, clapping their hands.

Goodness me! What large waves there were in that gutter, and what a strong current! —but then, it had been a real downpour. The paper boat was tossed up and down, and now and then turned round and round, until the tin soldier was quite dizzy. But he was brave and steadfast and didn't move a muscle. He just looked straight in front of him and shouldered his musket.

Suddenly the boat drifted into a long drainpipe, where it was just as dark as if he had been in his box. "Where am I going now?" he wondered. "This must be that goblin's doing. Now, if only the little maid were here in the boat with me, I would not mind it if it were twice as dark."

Just then a big water rat who lived in the drainpipe appeared.

"Where's your passport?" said the rat. "Let me see it."

The tin soldier said not a word and held his musket tighter than ever.

Away went the boat, and the rat after it. Ugh! How he gnashed his teeth as he shouted to sticks and straws, "Stop him! Stop him! He hasn't paid the toll! He hasn't shown his passport!"

But the current grew stronger and stronger. The tin soldier could now see daylight ahead, shining in at the end of the pipe. He could also hear a roar so loud it might easily have frightened the boldest man. For where the drainpipe ended, the water poured out into a large canal, and this was just as dangerous for the tin soldier as it would be for us to be carried over a great waterfall.

22

But by now he was so near that he could not stop. The boat shot out of the drainpipe into the canal. The poor tin soldier stiffened himself as well as he could, and no one could say that he even blinked an eye. The boat whirled around three or four times and filled with water. It would surely sink. The tin soldier stood up to his neck in water, the boat sank deeper and deeper, the paper fell to pieces more and more, and now the water closed over the soldier's head—and at that moment he thought of the charming little dancer whom he would never see again, and a song rang in his ears:

Forward, warrior, without fear,

Though, alas, your death is near.

Then the paper fell apart completely and the tin soldier sank down into the canal, where he was at once swallowed by a big fish. Oh, how dark it was in there! It was even worse than in the drainpipe, and there was so little room. But the tin soldier was steadfast and lay calmly at full length with his musket on his shoulder.

The fish darted about in the most alarming way, and then became quite still. After a long time, something suddenly flashed through it like lightning. Bright daylight appeared again, and someone shouted, "The tin soldier!" The fish had been caught, taken to market, sold, and brought to the kitchen, where the cook had cut it open with a big knife.

With two fingers she picked up the soldier by the waist and marched him into the sitting room, where everyone wanted to see this remarkable man who had been traveling about in the stomach of a fish. But the tin soldier did not let it go to his head. They stood him up on a table, and there—what curious things do happen in the world!—he was in the very same room where he had been before! He saw the very same boy, and the very same toys were standing on the table. There was the beautiful castle with the lovely little dancer in the doorway, still standing on one leg with the other held high up in the air. She too had remained steadfast. This touched the tin soldier so much that he almost wept tin tears, but of course that would not have been at all proper. He gazed at her and she gazed at him, but they said nothing.

Suddenly the little boy picked up the tin soldier and, without rhyme or reason, threw him into the fireplace. He never explained at all why he did it—it must have been the goblin in the snuffbox who was to blame.

The tin soldier stood there in the flames and felt a great heat, but whether it came from the fire or from his love he did not know. His bright colors had all faded away, but whether this had happened because of his journey or because of his grief no one could say.

He looked at the little dancer, and she looked at him. Though he felt himself melting, still he stood there bravely, shouldering his musket.

Suddenly the door flew open, a draft of air took hold of the dancer, and she flew like a sylph straight into the fireplace to the tin soldier, where she burst into flame and was gone.

The tin soldier melted down into a lump. Next morning, when the maid took out the ashes, she found him in the shape of a little tin heart. Of the dancer nothing was left but the sequin, which had been burned as black as coal. ❧

The Nightingale

It is many years now since this story happened, but that is all the more reason for telling it again, lest it be forgotten.

In China, there was once an emperor whose palace was the most magnificent in all the world. It was made entirely of porcelain—very costly, but so fragile that you had to be very careful how you touched it. In the garden were the most wonderful flowers, and tied to the most beautiful were silver bells, which tinkled so that no one should pass by without noticing them. Yes, everything in the emperor's garden was perfectly arranged, and it was so big that the gardener himself did not know where it ended.

If you kept on walking, you came into a glorious forest with tall trees and deep lakes. On one side the forest went straight down to the sea, which was blue and so deep that great ships could sail in right under the branches. In these branches lived a nightingale that sang so beautifully, even a poor fisherman, going out at night to cast his nets, stopped still to listen when he heard the nightingale. "How beautiful!" he said, but then he had to attend to his work and forgot the bird. Still, when the bird sang again the next night, the fisherman would once more exclaim, "How beautiful!"

Travelers from all the countries of the world came and admired the emperor's city, the palace, and the garden. But when they heard the nightingale, they all said, "That is the best thing of all!" And when they got home, they told of the nightingale. Learned people wrote many books about the town, palace, and garden, and they always mentioned the nightingale. And those who could write poetry wrote beautiful poems about the nightingale in the forest by the deep blue sea.

Those books were read all over the world, and in the course of time some of them reached the emperor. He sat in his golden chair and read and read, frequently nodding his head, for the delightful descriptions of his city, his palace, and his garden pleased him. "But the nightingale is the best of all," he read.

"What's this?" exclaimed the emperor. "The nightingale? I don't know anything about a nightingale! Is there such a bird in my empire, and even in my garden? I've never heard of it. Imagine having to learn about it from a book!"

And he sent for his chamberlain, who was so proud that when anyone of lower rank dared speak to him, he answered nothing but "P!"—and that meant nothing at all.

"There is said to be a wonderful bird in my garden called a nightingale!" said the emperor. "They say it's the finest thing in all my great empire. Why have I never heard anything about it?"

"I have never heard anyone mention it," replied the chamberlain. "It has never been introduced at court."

"I command that it appear this evening and sing for me," said the emperor. "I cannot have the whole world knowing what I possess when I do not know of it myself!"

"I have never heard any mention of it before," said the chamberlain, "but I shall seek it, and I shall find it."

But where was the bird to be found? The chamberlain ran up and down the staircases, through the halls and passages, asking about the bird. But not one of all those he asked had heard of the nightingale. So he ran back to the emperor and told him it must be some story made up by the people who wrote the books. "Your Imperial Majesty must not believe everything that is written. Books are often made up."

"But the book in which I read this was sent to me by the high and mighty Emperor of Japan," said the emperor. "Therefore it can't be made up. I insist on hearing the nightingale this evening! It shall enjoy my imperial favor! And if it doesn't come, the whole court shall be thumped in the stomach after supper."

"Tsing-pe!" said the chamberlain, and again he ran up and down all the staircases and through all the halls, and half the court ran with him, for the courtiers did not wish to have their stomachs thumped. And all of them kept asking about the remarkable nightingale that was known all over the world except at the emperor's court.

At last they found a poor little kitchen maid who said, "Oh, yes, the nightingale! I know it well. It sings gloriously. Every evening I am allowed to carry the table scraps to my poor, sick mother, who lives down by the shore. When I am on my way back and am tired, I rest in the forest, and then I hear the nightingale sing. It brings tears to my eyes, for it feels just like a kiss from my mother!"

"Little kitchen maid," said the chamberlain, "I will get you a better job in the kitchen, with permission to watch the emperor dine, if you will lead us to the nightingale, for it has been commanded to appear at court this evening."

So the kitchen maid, the chamberlain, and half the court all went to the forest where the nightingale usually sang, and as they were walking along, a cow began to moo.

"Oh!" cried the courtiers. "There it is! What a powerful voice from such a tiny creature! We have certainly heard it before."

"No, that's the cow mooing," said the little kitchen maid. "We are still a long way from the place."

Now the frogs began to croak in the marsh.

"Glorious!" said the court chaplain. "It sounds just like little church bells."

"No, those are frogs!" said the little kitchen maid. "But I think we'll be hearing it soon now."

And then the nightingale began to sing.

"That's it," said the little kitchen maid. "Listen, listen. And there it sits." And she pointed to a little gray bird up in the branches.

"Is it possible?" cried the chamberlain. "I should never have thought it looked like that! How ordinary it looks! It must have lost its color at seeing so many distinguished people around it."

"Little nightingale," called the kitchen maid quite loudly. "Our gracious emperor wishes you to sing before him."

"With the greatest pleasure," replied the nightingale, and it began to sing most delightfully.

"It sounds like crystal bells!" said the chamberlain. "And look at its little throat, how it throbs! It's amazing that we should never have heard it before. That bird will be a great success at court."

"Shall I sing once more for the emperor?" asked the nightingale, for it thought the emperor was present.

"My excellent little nightingale," said the chamberlain, "I have great pleasure in inviting you to a court banquet this evening, where you shall charm his Imperial Majesty with your beautiful singing."

"My song sounds best out here in the forest," replied the nightingale, but it went with them willingly when it heard that the emperor wished it.

The palace had been decorated for the occasion. The porcelain walls and floor gleamed in the light of thousands of golden lamps. The most beautiful flowers, each with its little bell, had been placed in the passages, and everyone was rushing about so much that all the bells began to ring. You could hardly hear yourself speak.

In the middle of the great hall where the emperor sat, a golden perch had been placed, and there the nightingale was to sit. The whole court was present, and the little kitchen maid had been permitted to stand behind the door, for now she had been given the title of Cook.

All were dressed in their finest clothes, and all were looking at the little gray bird as the emperor nodded for it to begin.

And the nightingale sang so beautifully that tears came into the emperor's eyes and ran down his cheeks. Then the nightingale sang even more sweetly, and its song went straight to the emperor's heart. The emperor was so pleased, he said the nightingale should have his golden slipper to wear around its neck. But the nightingale declined with thanks, for it had already been sufficiently rewarded.

27

"I have seen tears in the emperor's eyes," it said, "and that is the richest treasure, for an emperor's tears have a wondrous power. I have been rewarded enough." And then it sang again in its glorious voice.

"That is the sweetest thing I ever heard!" said the ladies, and they filled their mouths with water and tried to warble like the nightingale. Even the footmen and chambermaids were satisfied, and that is saying a good deal, for they are the most dif-ficult to please. In short, the nightingale was a great success.

It was decided that the nightingale would now remain at court, where it would have its own cage with the liberty to go out twice every day and once every night. Twelve servants were appointed to accompany the nightingale when it went out, each holding a silken ribbon fastened to the bird's leg. There was really no pleasure in an outing of that sort.

The entire city talked about the remarkable bird, and when two people met, one would simply say "Nightin," and the other "gale," and then they would sigh and understand one another. Eleven peddlers' children were named after the bird, but not one of them could sing a note.

One day the emperor received a large package with the word "Nightingale" written on it.

"Ah, we have been sent a new book about our celebrated bird," said the emperor. But it was not a book. It was a little work of art lying in a box, a mechanical nightingale exactly like the living one, except that it was studded all over with diamonds, rubies, and sapphires. When the mechanical bird was wound up, it sang one of the pieces that the real bird sang, then its tail wagged up and down, glittering with silver and gold. Round its neck hung a little ribbon, and on it was written, "The Emperor of Japan's nightingale is poor compared to that of the Emperor of China."

"How lovely!" everyone said, and the person who had brought the package immediately received the title of Imperial Nightingale Bringer.

"Now they must sing together—what a duet that will be!"

And so the birds had to sing together, but it did not go very well, for the real nightingale sang in its own way, and the mechanical bird sang only in waltz time.

"There is no fault in that," said the Court Music Master. "It is perfectly in time and it is correct in every way."

Then the mechanical bird was made to sing alone; it was admired just as much as the real bird and was much handsomer to look at, shining as it did like bracelets and brooches.

Thirty-three times it sang the same piece, and still it was not tired. The people would have gladly heard it again, but the emperor said that the living nightingale should be allowed to sing something now. But where was it? No one had noticed that it had flown, out the open window and back to its green forest.

"What is the meaning of this?" said the emperor. And all the courtiers grumbled and declared that the nightingale was a very ungrateful creature. "But we have the best bird," they said, and then the mechanical bird had to sing again. This was the thirty-fourth time they had listened to the same tune, but they did not know it by heart yet, for it was very difficult.

The music master praised the bird extravagantly and insisted that it was better than the real bird, not only on the outside, with all its jewels, but inside as well.

"For you see, ladies and gentlemen, and above all, your Imperial Majesty, with a real nightingale you never know what song is coming next, but with this mechanical bird the program is settled.

It will always work the same way. You can open it up and show people where the waltzes come from, how they go, how one note follows another."

"Those are our very thoughts," they all said, and the music master got permission to show the bird to the public the following Sunday. They were also to hear it sing, said the emperor. So the public heard the mechanical bird, and they were extremely pleased. They all said "Oooh!" and held up their forefingers and nodded.

But the poor fisherman, who had heard the real nightingale, said, "It sounds pretty enough, and it is very nearly like the real one, but there is something missing. I don't know what."

The real nightingale was banished from the empire, and the mechanical bird was placed on a silken cushion close to the emperor's bed. All the presents it had received, gold and precious jewels, were arranged around it, and its title was raised to Chief Imperial After-Dinner Singer. In rank it stood Number One on the left side, for the emperor considered the side on which the heart is found to be the most important, and even in an emperor the heart is on the left.

The music master wrote a work of twenty-five volumes about the mechanical bird. It was very learned, very long and full of the most difficult words, but all the people said they had read and understood it, for no one wanted to be thought stupid.

A whole year passed. The emperor, the court, and everyone in China knew every little twitter in the mechanical bird's song by then, but they liked it all the better for this, for they could all join in the song themselves. Even street boys sang "zee-zee-zee-cluck-cluck-cluck," and the emperor himself sang it, too.

But one evening, when the mechanical bird was singing its best, and the emperor lay in bed listening to it, something inside the bird went "Whizzz!" Something snapped. "Zip!" All the wheels went "whirrr," and then the music stopped.

The emperor sprang out of bed and summoned his doctor, but what could he do? Then he sent for the watchmaker, who, after a good deal of talk and examination, got the bird into some kind of order, but he warned that it must be treated very carefully, for its works were terribly worn, and if he replaced them the music might not play properly.

Then there was great sorrow at court. The mechanical bird was to be allowed to sing only once a year, and even that was almost too much. But then the music master made a little speech full of big words and said that everything was as good as before, and so everyone believed that everything was as good as before.

Five years passed, and a great grief came to the whole nation. The people really were fond of their emperor, and now he was ill and could not, it was said, live much longer.

The people stood out in the street and asked the chamberlain how their emperor was. "P!" he said, and shook his head.

Cold and pale, the emperor lay in his magnificent bed. The whole court thought he was dead, and they all ran off to pay their respects to a new emperor. The footmen ran outside to talk matters over, and the palace maids had a great coffee party. Everywhere, in all the halls and passages, cloth had been laid down so that no footstep could be heard, and so it was very, very quiet. But the emperor was not dead yet, though he lay stiff and pale on his gorgeous bed with its long velvet curtains and heavy gold tassels. High above him a window stood open, and the moon shone in on the emperor and the mechanical bird.

The poor emperor could hardly breathe; it felt as though he had a weight on his chest. He opened his eyes and saw that Death himself was sitting on his chest, and on his head was the emperor's golden crown. In one hand he held the emperor's sword and in the other his beautiful banner. And all around, in the folds of the velvet curtains, strange heads peered forth. A few were very ugly, but the rest were quite lovely. These were all the emperor's bad and good deeds, standing before him now that Death sat upon his heart.

"Do you remember this?" whispered one to another. "Do you remember that?" Then they reminded him of so many things that perspiration ran from his forehead.

"I don't remember!" cried the emperor. "Music, music! The great Chinese drum!" he shouted, "so I don't have to hear what they are saying!" But they went on and on, as Death sat nodding at everything they said.

"Music, music!" cried the emperor again. "Precious golden bird, sing, sing! I have given you gold and costly presents, even hung my golden slipper around your neck! Now sing, sing!"

But the bird remained silent. No one was there to wind it up, and it could not sing without that. But Death continued to stare at the Emperor with his great hollow eyes, and everything was quiet, so fearfully quiet!

Then suddenly, from outside the window, came the loveliest song. It was the little live nightingale, perched on a branch outside. It had heard of the emperor's distress and had

come to sing to him of comfort and hope. And as it sang, the strange faces around the emperor's bed grew paler and paler, and the blood ran more quickly through the emperor's weak limbs, and even Death himself listened and said, "Go on, little nightingale, go on!"

"But will you give me that splendid golden sword? Will you give me that rich banner? Will you give me the emperor's crown?"

And Death gave up each of these treasures for a song, and the nightingale sang on and on. It sang of the quiet churchyard where the white roses grow, where the elder blossom smells sweet, and where the fresh grass is watered by tears. Then Death felt a longing for his own garden, and he slipped away out the window like a cold white mist.

"Thank you, thank you!" said the emperor. "You heavenly little bird! I know you well! I banished you from my empire, and yet you have charmed the evil visions from my bed and banished Death from my heart! How can I reward you?"

"You have already rewarded me," replied the nightingale. "I brought tears to your eyes the very first time I ever sang for you, and I shall never forget that. Those are the jewels that gladden a singer's heart. But sleep now and grow fresh and strong again. I will sing to you."

And it sang, and the emperor fell into a sweet slumber. Ah! How mild and refreshing that sleep was. And when he awoke, the sun shone upon him through the windows and he was strong and well. Not one of his servants had yet returned, for they all thought he was dead, but the nightingale still sat there singing.

"You must stay with me always!" said the emperor. "You shall sing only when you please, and I will break the mechanical bird into a thousand pieces."

"Don't do that," replied the nightingale. "It did well as long as it could. Keep it as you have always done. I cannot build my nest and live in this palace, but let me come when I please. Then I will sit in the evening on the branch by the window and sing to you. I will sing to cheer you and to make you thoughtful. I will sing of those who are happy and of those who suffer. I will sing of the good and the evil hidden round about you. A little songbird must fly far and wide, to the poor fisherman, to the peasant's roof, to those who dwell far away from you and your court. But I love your heart more than your crown, and I will come and sing to you. But one thing you must promise me."

"Anything!" said the emperor, standing in his imperial robes, which he had put on himself, and pressing the heavy gold sword to his heart.

"One thing I beg of you. Tell no one that you have a little bird who tells you everything. It will be better that way."

Then the nightingale flew away.

And when the servants came in to look after their dead emperor, they found him standing there. And the emperor said, "Good morning." ⚘

The Princess and the Pea

There was once a prince who wanted to marry a princess, but she had to be a real princess. He traveled all over the world to find one, but though there were plenty of princesses, there always seemed to be something wrong with them. He could never be certain that they were *real* princesses. And so he came home again, feeling very sad, for he so much wanted to marry a true princess.

Then one night a terrible storm arose. The wind howled. Thunder crashed, lightning flashed, and rain poured down in torrents. In the middle of the storm, there came a knock at the castle gate, and the old king, the prince's father, went out to open it.

Outside the gate stood a princess, but she hardly looked like one! Water streamed from her hair and clothes. It ran in through the toes of her shoes and out through the heels. The fierce storm had treated her very roughly. Still, she said she was a real princess. So the old king brought her in to meet the queen.

"A real princess?" thought the queen. "Well, we'll soon find out." But she said nothing. Instead she summoned the maids to prepare a bedroom for the girl. First they removed all the bedding, and then the queen placed a single pea on the bed. Then they laid twenty mattresses on top of the pea, and twenty eiderdown quilts on top of the mattresses. And there, on top of it all, the princess was sent to sleep that night.

In the morning, the old queen asked her how she had slept.

"Oh, very badly indeed," said the tired princess. "I got scarcely a wink of sleep all night! Heaven only knows what was in the bed, but I seemed to be lying on something very, very hard, and now my whole body is black and blue this morning. It was just dreadful!" she exclaimed.

Then they all knew that this was a real princess, for she had felt the pea through twenty mattresses and twenty eiderdown quilts, and no one else could be so delicate. So the prince asked her to be his wife, for he knew he had found a true princess at last. And the pea was placed in the royal museum, where it may still be seen today, unless someone has taken it.

The Little Mermaid

Far out in the ocean the water is as blue as the loveliest cornflower and as clear as the purest glass, but it is very deep — much deeper than any anchor chain can reach, and many church steeples would have to be placed one on top of the other to stretch from the ocean bottom to the surface above. Down there live the sea folk.

Now, you must not imagine that there is only bare white sand at the bottom. The most wonderful trees and plants grow there, with stalks and leaves so supple that they move with the slightest motion of the water. And in and out among the branches dart fishes, large and small, just like birds in the trees.

In the very deepest spot lies the sea king's palace. Its walls are made of coral, its tall windows are of the clearest amber, and its roof is of mussel shells that open and shut as the water flows over them. They are beautiful to see, for in each shell lies a gleaming pearl, any one of which would be a treasure fit for a queen's crown.

The sea king had been a widower for many years, and his old mother kept house for him. She was a clever woman, but very proud of her royal birth, so she always wore twelve oysters on her tail, whereas others of high rank were allowed to wear only six.

Otherwise she deserved nothing but praise, especially for the love she felt for the little sea princesses, her granddaughters.

There were six of them, each one a beautiful child, but the youngest was the prettiest of them all. Her skin was as delicate as a rose and her eyes were as blue as the deep sea, but, like the others, she had no feet, for her body ended in a fish tail. All day long the princesses played in the spacious halls of the castle, where living flowers grew on the walls. When the large amber windows were opened, the fish swam in to eat from the girls' hands and let themselves be petted.

Outside the castle was a large garden with fiery red and dark blue trees. Their fruits shone like gold and their flowers like burning fire as their stalks and leaves swayed to and fro in the water. The ground itself was the finest sand, but blue as burning brimstone. A wonderful blue glow shone over everything, so that you might think you were high in the air, with nothing but blue sky above and beneath you, instead of at the bottom of the sea. In calm weather you could

see the sun, which looked like a crimson flower high above, streaming light over the world.

Each of the princesses had her own special spot in the garden, where she could dig and plant just as she pleased. One made her garden in the shape of a whale, another in the shape of a mermaid, but the youngest made hers as round as the sun and grew only flowers that shone red like the sun. She was a curious child, quiet and thoughtful, and when her sisters decorated their gardens with wonderful things they had found in sunken ships, she decorated hers with only a marble statue—a beautiful figure of a charming boy. It was carved out of pure, white stone and had sunk from a wreck to the bottom of the sea. Beside it she planted a rose-colored weeping willow, which grew splendidly. Its branches drooped over the statue and were reflected in purple shadows on the sandy blue seabed, so that with every movement of the branches it looked as if the tree and its roots were kissing each other.

Nothing pleased the little princess more than to hear about the world above the sea, and she made her grandmother tell her everything she knew about ships and towns and people and animals. It amazed her to hear that on land flowers had fragrance (at the bottom of the sea they have no scent at all), and that the forest was green, and fish sang! (It was the birds that the grandmother called fish, for they flew about the trees on land just as the fish swam about the trees in the sea.)

"When you are fifteen years old," their grandmother told the princesses, "I will let you go up to the surface and sit on the rocks in the moonlight, and watch the great ships go sailing by. Then you will see the forests and the towns for yourself."

The oldest princess would turn fifteen the following year. Each sister was a year younger than the next, so the youngest had six whole years to wait. The oldest, however, promised to tell the others everything she saw, for their grandmother could never tell them enough, and there was so much they wanted to know.

None of them, though, was as filled with longing as the youngest, who had the longest to wait and was so quiet and thoughtful. Many nights she stood by the open window and looked up through the dark blue water, where the fish were swimming about, to the moon and stars shining faintly above. Through the water they looked much larger to the little princess than they do to us, and if now and then a black cloud seemed to glide beneath them, she knew that it was either a whale swimming above her or a ship filled with people who never imagined that a lovely little mermaid was standing beneath them, stretching her white hands toward the keel.

When the oldest princess turned fifteen, she went up to the surface. She came back with a hundred things to tell, but the most beautiful thing of all, she said, was to lie in the moonlight on a sandbank in the calm sea, and watch the great town on shore where the lights blinked like hundreds of stars, to hear the music and the clamor of all the carriages and people, and to see all the church towers and spires and hear the bells ringing. And because she could not go there herself, the youngest sister longed all the more to see these things.

Oh, how eagerly she listened, and when she stood at night by the open window and looked up through the dark blue water, she thought of that town with its noise and bustle and fancied that she too could hear the ringing of the bells.

The next year the second sister was allowed to swim up to the surface. She rose up just as the sun was setting, and this, she thought, was the most beautiful sight of all. The whole sky had looked like gold, and the clouds—well, she simply could not describe their beauty. Red and violet, they drifted over her. Far faster than the clouds, a flock of wild swans flew like a long white veil over the water toward the setting sun. She swam toward them, but the sun sank and the rosy glow on the clouds and sea vanished.

The next year the third sister went up. She was the boldest of them all, and she swam right up a broad river that ran to the sea. There she saw lovely green hills covered with vines. Palaces and farms were nestled in grand forests. She heard birds singing, and the sun shone so warmly that she had to dart down under the water to cool her burning face.

In one little bay she found a crowd of children running about naked and splashing in the water. She wanted to play with them, but they ran off, frightened, and a little black animal— it was a dog, but she had never before seen a dog—barked at her so furiously that she too became frightened and swam back to the open sea. But she would never be able to forget the beautiful forests, the green hills, and the pretty children who could swim in the water even though they had no fish tails.

The fourth sister was not so bold. She stayed out in the open sea, and she told them that was the loveliest place of all. You could see for miles around, and the sky above looked like a huge glass dome. She had seen ships, but they were so far away they looked like seagulls. The dolphins had turned somersaults, and the great whales had spouted water from their blowholes so that it looked like hundreds of fountains all around.

Now came the turn of the fifth sister. Her birthday was in the winter, so she saw things on her first trip that the others had not. The sea looked quite green, and large icebergs floated all around. They looked like pearls, she said, but they were far taller than the church towers built by people, and they took the most wonderful shapes and glittered just like diamonds. She had climbed up on one of the largest, but all the ships had steered away in terror from where she sat, her long hair floating in the wind.

Later the sky filled with clouds, lightning flashed, and thunder rolled. The black sea tossed huge blocks of ice into the air, where they glistened in the flashes of lightning. On all the ships the sails were furled in terror, but she sat quietly on her floating iceberg and watched the zigzag flashes of blue lightning disappear into the sea.

When the sisters first went up to the surface of the ocean, each was delighted with the new and beautiful things she saw, but after a time they grew indifferent. Now that they could visit the upper world whenever they liked, they soon lost interest. They said it was much more beautiful down below, and besides, it was so nice to be home. Still, on many evenings the five sisters went up to the surface, arm in arm. They had beautiful voices, more beautiful than any human being, and when a storm was brewing and they thought that ships were sure to be wrecked, they swam in front of them and sang about how beautiful it was at the bottom of the sea and begged the sailors not to fear coming down. But the sailors could not understand their songs and thought they were only the whistling of the storm. Nor could they ever see the splendors below, for if their ship went down, they drowned and sank only as dead men to the sea king's palace.

On the evenings when her sisters rose up arm in arm through the sea, the littlest mermaid stood alone gazing after them. She looked as if she might cry, but a mermaid has no tears, and so she suffers all the more.

"Oh, if only I were fifteen!" she cried. "I know I will love the world above and the people who live there."

Finally her fifteenth birthday came.

"Well, at last you are of age," said her grandmother. "Come, let me dress you up prettily like your sisters." And she put a wreath of white lilies in the girl's hair, but each petal in the flowers was half a pearl. Then the old lady had eight big oysters pinch onto the princess's tail to show her high rank.

"They hurt!" cried the little mermaid.

"Yes, but you must suffer if you want to look nice," said her grandmother.

Oh, what would she not have given to shake off all this oyster finery and lay aside this heavy crown. The red flowers in her garden suited her much better, but she had no choice in the matter.

"Goodbye," she said, and she rose, as light and clear as a bubble, up through the sea.

The sun had just set when she raised her head above the sea's surface, but the clouds were still tinged with gold and rose, and high up in the pale pink sky, the evening star shone bright and beautiful. The sea was calm and the air was mild and fresh. Nearby lay a great ship with three masts, but only one sail was set, for there was scarcely a breath of wind, and the sailors were sitting in the shrouds and on the yards. There was music and singing, and as the night grew darker, hundreds of colored lanterns were lit, and it looked as if the flags of every nation were fluttering in the air.

The little mermaid swam up close to the cabin porthole, and whenever the waves lifted her up, she looked in through the clear glass panes. Inside, people were standing about, dressed in their best. The handsomest of them was a young prince with large black eyes, who couldn't have been more than sixteen years old. In fact, today was his birthday, and that was the reason for all the festivity. The sailors were dancing on the deck, and when the young prince came out of the cabin, hundreds of rockets blazed up into the air, lighting up the scene as bright as day. The little mermaid was so frightened, she dived under the water. But she soon came up again, and then it seemed as if all the stars of heaven were raining down upon her. Never had she seen such splendor. Great suns were spinning around, wondrous fire fishes hovered in the air, and everything was brilliantly reflected in the clear, calm sea. The ship itself was so brightly lit that she could clearly see all the people and even every little bit of rope. Oh, how handsome the young prince was as he shook hands with the sailors, smiled, and laughed, while sweet strains of music floated into the soft night air.

It was getting late, but the little mermaid could not take her eyes away from the ship and the beautiful prince. The colored lanterns were put out, the rockets no longer shot into the air, and the cannons had ceased firing, but deep down in the sea there was a moaning and a rumbling. The little mermaid was rocking up and down on the waves so she could see into the cabin. Then the waves rose higher, heavy clouds gathered, and lightning flashed in the distance. A terrible storm was approaching.

Suddenly the ship was plunging wildly through a raging sea. Waves rose like great dark mountains as if to hurl themselves over the masts, but like a swan the ship ducked down between them, then rose again on their lofty crests. To the little mermaid it all looked like fun, but the sailors thought differently. The ship groaned and creaked, the main mast snapped in two like a reed, the thick planks gave way to the pounding of the sea, and the ship leaned over on its side as water rushed into the hold.

Now the little mermaid saw that the ship was in danger, and she herself had to watch out for the wreckage that was drifting about. One moment it was pitch-dark and she could see nothing at all, but when lightning flashed, the ship was brilliantly lit and she could see

everyone on board. Each was struggling as best he could, but where was the young prince? At last, as the ship broke apart, she saw him sinking into the deep sea.

At first she was delighted, for now he was going down into her realm. But then she remembered that human beings cannot survive in the water, so that when he got down to her father's palace he would certainly be dead.

No! He must not die! Without even thinking of the danger, she swam about the ship's wreckage, now diving deep down into the water, now rising high up on the waves. In this way she at last came to the young prince, who could hardly swim any longer in the raging sea. His arms and legs had begun to fail him, and his beautiful eyes were closed. He would surely have died had the little mermaid not reached him. She held his head above the water and let the waves carry them wherever they wished.

In the morning the storm was over, but there was no trace of the ship. The sun rose red and glowing from the sea, and it seemed to bring life back to the prince's cheeks, though his eyes remained closed. The mermaid kissed his forehead and stroked his wet hair. He looked like the marble statue in her garden, she thought, and she kissed him again and hoped that he would live.

Ahead she saw land. Lofty blue mountains rose in the distance, their snowy peaks shining like a flock of white swans. Along the coast was a beautiful green wood, and nestled among the trees was a building of some kind—a church or a convent, she did not know which. In its garden were orange and citron trees, and tall palms grew by its gates. Here the sea formed a little bay where the water was calm, and there she swam with the handsome prince and laid him on the sand, taking care that his head should lie in the warm sunshine.

Then the bells in the big white building began to ring, and a crowd of young girls came out into the garden. So the little mermaid swam out into the bay, hid herself behind some high rocks, and covered herself with sea foam, so she could not be seen. From there she watched to see who would come to find the poor prince.

Before long a young girl approached. At first she seemed frightened, but only for a moment. Then she ran to get help. The mermaid saw the prince awaken and smile at everyone around him, but he did not smile out at her, for of course he did not know that she had saved him. She felt very sad, and when he was taken into the big white building, she dived mournfully beneath the waves and made her way back to her father's palace.

She had always been quiet and thoughtful, but now she became even more so. Her sisters asked her what she had seen on her first trip to the surface, but she told them nothing.

Many mornings and evenings she swam up to the place where she had left the prince. She saw the snow melt on the lofty mountains, she saw the fruits in the garden ripen and be plucked, but she never saw the prince, and so she always went home more unhappy than ever.

Her only comfort was to sit in her little garden and throw her arms around the beautiful statue that looked like the prince. But she no longer tended her flowers, and they grew in confusion over the paths and trailed their long stems and leaves up into the tree branches, so that the whole garden grew quite dark and gloomy.

At last she could keep her secret no longer and told it to one of her sisters, who told it to the rest. No one else was told except one or two other mermaids, who told no one but their dearest friends. One of these had also seen the festivities on the ship, and she knew who the prince was and where he came from.

"Come, little sister," said the other princesses, and arm in arm they rose up to the surface close to where the prince's palace stood.

The palace was built of pale yellow stone, with large flights of marble steps, one of which led right down to the sea. Magnificent golden domes rose above the roof, and between the columns that surrounded the building stood marble statues that looked as real as life. Through the tall windows the mermaids could see into magnificent halls hung with costly silk curtains, tapestries and beautiful paintings. In the middle of the grandest hall was a large fountain. From it jets of water rose high up toward a glass dome in the ceiling, through which the sun shone on the water and on the beautiful plants growing in the large pool below.

Now that the little mermaid knew where the prince lived, she spent many evenings there, swimming much closer to the land than any of the others had dared. She even went right up the narrow canal beneath a splendid marble balcony that cast a long shadow upon the water. Hidden there, she sat gazing at the young prince, who thought he was quite alone in the moonlight. On many evenings she saw him sailing with his musicians in a magnificent boat, its flags waving in the breeze. She peered out through the reeds, and anyone who saw the wind catch her long silvery veil thought it was only a swan spreading its wings.

Many nights, when the fishermen cast their nets by torchlight, she overheard them telling each other many good things about the prince, and she was happy to think that she had saved his life when he was drifting half dead on the waves. She remembered how his head had rested on her shoulder and how tenderly she had kissed him. But he knew nothing at all of this, and did not even dream of her existence.

Day by day human beings became more dear to her, and more and more she wished she could live among them. Their world seemed so much larger than her own, for they could fly across the sea in ships, could climb lofty mountains higher than the clouds, and the land they owned stretched through fields and forests farther than her eye could see.

"If human beings don't drown," the little mermaid asked her old grandmother, "do they live forever? Do they not die, as we die down here in the sea?"

"Yes," replied the old lady, "they too must die, and their lifetime is much shorter than ours. We can live three hundred years, but when we die, we become merely foam on the water and do not even have a grave among our loved ones. We have no immortal soul—for us there is no life hereafter. We are like the green rushes that, once cut down, are never green again. Human beings, on the other hand, each have a soul that lives forever, even after their bodies have turned to dust. It rises up through the air to the shining stars. Just as we rise up from the sea to see the land above, so they rise up to unknown beautiful places that we can never see."

"Why were we not given immortal souls?" asked the little mermaid in distress. "I would give all the three hundred years that I have to live, just to be a human being for a single day and then share in the heavenly world."

"You mustn't think that way," said the grandmother. "We have far better and happier lives down here than the human beings have up there."

"So I must die and float as foam upon the sea, and never again hear the music of the waves or see the beautiful flowers and the bright sun! Can I do nothing to gain an immortal soul?"

"No," said the old lady. "Only if a human being were to love you so dearly that you meant more to him than his father or mother. Only if he clung to you with all his heart and all his mind, and married you, promising to be faithful to you now and through all eternity. Then his soul would flow into you. He would give you a soul but still keep his own, and you would share the happiness of humankind. But that can never happen, for your fish tail, which we think so beautiful down here in the sea, is thought to be ugly up on earth, for they know no better. There, to be pretty, you must have two clumsy sticks that they call legs."

The little mermaid looked sadly at her fish tail and sighed.

"Let us be contented," said the grandmother. "Let us enjoy ourselves for the three hundred years we have to live—that is quite a long time, you know. And tonight there is a ball at court."

The court ball was more splendid than anything ever seen on earth. The ballroom walls and ceiling were made of thick glass. Hundreds of colossal mussel shells, rose pink and grass green, were arranged in rows on either side. They gave forth a bluish light that lit the whole room and shone through the walls to light up the sea outside. You could see countless fish, both large and small, swimming toward the glass walls, some flashing in purple hues, others glittering like silver and gold. A broad stream flowed through the center of the hall, and in it the mermen and mermaids danced to the music of their own lovely singing. No one on earth ever had such a beautiful voice, and the little princess sang most sweetly of all. Everyone applauded her, so that for a moment her heart felt light. But she could not forget the handsome prince for long, or her grief at not having an immortal soul like his, so in the midst of the merriment she crept out of her father's palace to sit, full of sorrow, in her little garden.

Suddenly she heard horns sounding down through the water, and she thought, "He is sailing up there, the prince I love more than my father and mother, the prince who fills my thoughts and into whose hands I would gladly lay my life's happiness. I would risk everything to win him and an immortal soul. While my sisters are dancing in my father's palace, I will go to the sea witch. Though I have always been afraid of her, she may be able to help me."

So the little mermaid left her garden and swam toward the foaming whirlpools behind which the sea witch lived. She had never been there before. There were no flowers, there was no grass, only a stretch of bare gray sand leading toward the whirlpools, where the current spun round and round like whirling mill wheels, dragging everything within reach down into the deep. She knew she had to go through these rushing whirlpools to reach the place where the sea witch lived, and for a long way the only path led over hot bubbling mud, which the witch called her peat bog. Beyond it stood her house, in the middle of a gruesome forest in which all the trees and bushes were half animal and half plant. They looked like snakes with hundreds of heads growing out of the ground. Their branches were long slimy arms with fingers like worms, and they wriggled from their roots to their outermost tips, twining themselves around anything they could catch. When once in their grasp, nothing ever escaped.

The little mermaid was terrified and her heart pounded in fear. She was at the point of going back, but then she remembered the prince and the human soul, and this gave her courage. So she wound her long floating hair around her head so the beasts couldn't grab hold of it. Then, crossing her hands over her chest, she darted like a fish through the water in between the monsters, which reached out for her with their curling arms and fingers. She saw that every one of them was holding onto something it had caught with arms as strong as iron bands. Human beings who had drowned and sunk to the bottom of the sea were now white skeletons held in the arms of the beasts. Ship rudders and treasure chests and bones of land animals were held fast in their embrace.

Then she came to a large slimy open place in the forest where huge water snakes were crawling about, showing their ugly yellow bellies. In the middle of the clearing, a house had been built with the white bones of shipwrecked sailors, and there sat the sea witch, with a crab eating out of her mouth. The hideous water snakes she called her little chicks, and she let them crawl about on her big slimy chest.

"I know exactly what you want," said the sea witch, "and it is very stupid of you, for it will bring you misfortune, my beautiful princess. But even so, you shall have your way. You want to get rid of your fish tail, and instead have two sticks to walk on like human beings, so that the young prince can fall in love with you and you can have him and an immortal soul." And the witch laughed so loudly and horribly that the crab and the sea snakes fell writhing to the seafloor. "I will make a potion for you. Before the sun rises you must swim to land, sit down on the shore, and drink it. Then your fish tail will divide and shrink into what people of earth call legs. But the change will be very painful—you will feel as if you are being stabbed with a sharp sword. Everyone who sees you will say you are the most beautiful creature they have ever seen, and you will be as graceful as ever. No dancer will ever move so elegantly, but every step you take will be as painful as if you were treading on daggers. If you choose to suffer all this, I will help you."

"Yes," said the little mermaid in a trembling voice, thinking of the prince and of winning an immortal soul.

"But remember," said the witch, "once you have taken human form, you can never become a mermaid again. You will never be able to go down through the water to your sisters or to visit your father's palace. And if you do not succeed in winning the love of the prince so that for your sake he forgets father and mother, if he does not love you with all his heart and take you for his wife, you can never receive an immortal soul. The morning after he marries another, your heart will break, and you will become nothing but foam on the sea."

"I am willing!" said the little mermaid, turning deathly pale.

"But I must also be paid," said the witch, "and it is no small thing that I shall ask of you. You have the most beautiful voice of all down here at the bottom of the sea. You think you'll be able to charm your prince with that, but you must give that voice to me. For my precious potion, I must have the best thing you possess, for I must mix my own blood into it so that it will be as keen as a double-edged sword."

"But when you take my voice," said the little mermaid, "what shall I have left?"

"Your beautiful figure," said the witch, "your graceful movements, and your eloquent eyes. With these you can surely enchant a man's heart. Well, have you lost your courage?"

"So be it," said the little mermaid, and the witch put her cauldron on the fire to make the magic potion.

"Cleanliness is good," the sea witch said, and wiping out the cauldron with the snakes, which she had twisted into a knot. Then she scratched her chest and let her black blood drip down into it. The steam took such horrible shapes that anyone would have been terrified at the sight. The witch tossed more and more ingredients into the cauldron, and when it boiled it made a sound like crocodiles weeping. When at last the potion was ready, it looked like the purest water.

"Here you are," said the witch. From then on, the little mermaid could neither speak nor sing.

"If the beasts should grab you as you go back through the forest," said the witch, "you need only throw one drop of this potion on them, and their arms and fingers will break into a thousand pieces."

But the little mermaid had no need to do that, for the beasts drew back in terror when they saw the shining potion glittering in her hands like a star. And so she soon passed through the forest, the marsh, and the rushing whirlpools.

When she came to her father's palace, the torches in the ballroom were all out. Probably everyone was asleep, but still she did not dare go to see them, now that she could not speak

and was about to leave them forever. She felt as if her heart would break with grief. She crept out into the garden, picked one single blossom from each of her sisters' flower beds, blew a thousand kisses toward the palace, then rose up through the deep blue sea.

The sun had not yet risen when she came to the prince's palace and pulled herself up the splendid marble steps, and the moon was shining bright and clear as she drank the sharp, burning potion. It felt as if a double-edged sword had slashed right through her delicate body, and she fainted and lay as if dead. When she awoke, the sun was shining over the sea. She felt a searing pain, but just in front of her stood the handsome young prince with his beautiful black eyes fixed on her. She looked down and saw that her fish tail was gone. In its place were the loveliest legs any girl could have, but she was quite naked, so she wrapped herself in her long thick hair. The prince asked her who she was and where she came from, and she looked at him so sweetly, but oh so sadly, for she could not speak. He took her by the hand and led her into the palace, and with every step she felt as if she were walking on sharp knives, just as the witch had foretold, but she suffered it gladly. She moved as lightly as a bubble by the prince's side, and everyone marveled at her grace.

They dressed her in costly silks, and in the palace she was the most beautiful of them all, but she could neither speak nor sing. Lovely dancing girls dressed in silver and gold sang for the prince and his royal parents. One of them sang more beautifully than the others, and the prince clapped his hands and smiled at her. This made the little mermaid sad, for she knew she could once have sung far more sweetly. "If only he could know that to be with him I have given away my voice forever," she thought.

The dancing girls performed pretty fairylike dances to the sweetest music. Then the little mermaid raised her lovely white arms and floated across the floor on the tips of her toes, dancing as no one had ever danced before. With every exquisite movement her beauty became more stunning, and her eyes spoke more eloquently to the heart than the songs of the dancing girls. Everyone was charmed, especially the prince, who called her his little foundling. So she danced again and again, though each time her foot touched the floor it felt as if she were stepping on sharp knives.

The prince said she should be with him always, and she was allowed to sleep on a velvet cushion outside his door. He had clothes made for her so that she could go riding with him, and they rode through sweet-scented woods where the green boughs swept her shoulders and the little birds sang. With the prince she climbed the lofty mountains, and although her delicate feet bled, she only smiled, and they climbed on until they saw the clouds floating beneath them like a flock of birds flying to foreign lands.

At home in the prince's palace, when all were asleep at night, she went out on the broad marble steps and cooled her burning feet in the cold seawater and thought of her home down there in the depths of the sea.

One night her sisters came up arm in arm, singing mournfully as they swam along. She waved to them, and they recognized her and told her how sad she had made them all. After that

53

they came to visit every night, and once, far out on the waves, she saw her old grandmother, who had not been up to the surface for many years. The sea king was there too, wearing his crown. They stretched their arms toward her, but didn't dare come as close to land as her sisters.

Day by day, the prince grew fonder of the little mermaid. He loved her as one loves a sweet child, but it never occurred to him to make her his wife. And yet she had to become his wife or she would never have an immortal soul, but would turn into foam on the water on the morning after his wedding.

"Do you not love me best of all?" the little mermaid's eyes seemed to say when he took her in his arms and kissed her beautiful forehead.

"Yes, you are the one I love most," said the prince, "for you have the kindest heart of them all. You are the most devoted to me, and you remind me of a young maid I once met but shall probably never see again. My ship had wrecked, and the waves carried me to land near a holy temple, where several young girls were serving. The youngest of them found me on the shore and saved my life. I saw her only twice, but she is the only one in the world I could love. You look very like her—you have almost driven her image from my mind. She belongs to the holy temple, and so you have been sent to me instead, and we will never part."

"He does not know that I saved his life," thought the little mermaid. "I carried him over the sea to the forest where the temple stands. I sat behind the foam and watched to see whether anyone would come to his aid." And the mermaid sighed deeply, for she could not weep. "The girl belongs to the holy temple, he says. She will never come out into the world, and they will never meet again. But I am with him and see him every day. I will take care of him, love him, give my life for him."

Now people began to say that the prince was about to marry the beautiful daughter of a neighboring king, and that was why such a splendid ship was being fitted out. The prince, it was announced, was going to visit the neighboring king's country. But everyone knew that he was really going to see the princess.

The little mermaid shook her head and smiled, for she knew the prince's thoughts better than anyone. "My parents wish me to meet the beautiful princess," he had told her, "and so I must. But they do not insist that I bring her back home as my bride, and I cannot love her. She isn't the girl in the temple, the one you resemble. If I ever choose a bride, I would rather choose you, my silent foundling with talking eyes." And he kissed her rosy lips and played with her long hair and laid his head on her heart, while she dreamed of human happiness and an immortal soul.

"You are surely not afraid of the sea, my dear silent child?" he said as they stood on the magnificent ship that was to carry them to the country of the neighboring king. And he told her of storms and calms, of the strange fish in the deep, and of what divers had seen there. She smiled at his stories, for she knew better than anyone the wonders at the bottom of the sea.

In the moonlight, when all were asleep, she stood by the ship railings staring down though the clear water, and it seemed to her that she could see her father's palace.

Her old grandmother was standing on top of it, a silver crown on her head, gazing up through the waves toward the keel of the ship. Then her sisters came up to the surface and looked at her sadly and wrung their hands. She beckoned to them, smiling, and wanted to tell them how happy she was, but a cabin boy came along, and her sisters dived below, so he thought that all he had seen was the foam of the sea.

The next morning the ship sailed into the harbor of the neighboring kingdom. All the church bells were ringing, and trumpets were blown from the high towers while soldiers stood at attention down below, their bayonets glittering and their colors flying.

Every day was a festival. Balls and receptions followed one upon the other, but the princess was not there yet. She was being educated far away in a holy temple, where she was learning all the royal virtues. But at last she arrived.

The little mermaid was there, anxious to see whether she was as beautiful as she was said to be, and she had to acknowledge that she had never seen a lovelier creature. Her skin was so soft and clear, and behind her long black eyelashes smiled two faithful blue eyes.

"It was you," said the prince, "you who saved me when I lay dying by the shore!" And he folded his blushing bride in his arms. "Oh, I am so happy," he told the little mermaid. "That which I wished for most but never dared to hope for has come to pass. I know you will rejoice at my happiness, for you love me best of all." And the little mermaid kissed his hand, but she felt as if her heart were breaking.

Heralds rode through the streets to proclaim the royal wedding, and all the church bells rang out. Sweet-smelling oil burned in silver lamps on all the altars. The priests swung their incense burners, and the bride and bridegroom joined their hands and received the bishop's blessing. The little mermaid stood in silk and gold and held the bride's train, but her ears didn't hear the festive music and her eyes didn't see the holy ceremony. She was thinking of her death, and of what she had lost in this world.

That very same night the bride and groom went on board the ship. The cannon sounded and all the flags waved in the evening breeze. In the middle of the ship stood a royal tent of gold and purple, filled with the softest cushions. Here the bridal couple was to sleep.

The sails swelled in the wind, and the ship glided smoothly out of the harbor and over the clear sea. When it grew dark, colorful lanterns were lit, and the crew danced merrily on deck. The little mermaid couldn't help but think of the first time she rose up to the surface of the sea and saw the same joy and splendor, and she whirled around in the dance, floating like a swallow, and everyone cheered in admiration, for she had never danced so beautifully. Her tender feet were as if cut by sharp knives, but she did not feel it, for a sharper pain pierced her heart. She knew this was the last evening she would see the prince for whom she had left her family and her home, sacrificed her beautiful voice, and suffered so much pain of which he knew nothing. It was the last night she would breathe the same air as he and behold the same blue sea and starry sky. Instead an everlasting night without thoughts or dreams awaited her, for she had no soul and now could never win one.

The merrymaking continued until long past midnight, and the mermaid smiled and danced with the thought of death in her heart. The prince kissed his beautiful bride, and she caressed his coal black hair, and arm in arm they went to rest in the gorgeous tent.

Silence fell on the ship, and only the first mate stood at the helm. The little mermaid leaned on the railing and looked toward the east, watching for the rosy dawn that she knew would kill her. Then she saw her sisters rise from the sea. They were as pale as she, but their long beautiful hair floated no more in the wind—it had been cut off.

"We have given it to the sea witch," they said, "to win her help so you won't have to die tonight. She has given us a knife—here it is. Look how sharp it is. Before the sun rises, you must plunge it into the prince's heart, and when his warm blood splashes on your feet they will grow together back into a fish tail. You will be a mermaid again and can come home with us and live your three hundred years before you turn into sea foam. Hurry! Either he or you must die before sunrise. Our old grandmother is so upset that her white hair has fallen out just as ours fell to the witch's scissors. Kill the prince and come home! Hurry! Already there's a touch of red in the sky. In a few minutes the sun will rise, and it will be too late!" And they sighed deeply and sank beneath the waves.

The little mermaid drew the purple curtain back from the tent and saw the lovely bride sleeping with her head on the prince's breast. Kneeling down, she kissed his noble forehead. The morning sky was growing lighter. She looked at the dagger in her hand, then back at the prince, who in his dreams whispered his bride's name: she alone was in his thoughts. The

knife trembled in the mermaid's hand. She threw
it far out into the waves, which turned red where
it fell, as though drops of blood were bubbling up
through the water. She gazed at the prince one
last time. Then she threw herself from the ship
down into the sea, where she felt her body
dissolving into foam.

The sun rose from the sea. Its rays fell warm
and gentle on the cold sea foam, and the little
mermaid had no sense of dying. She saw the
shining sun, and up above her hovered hundreds
of beautiful transparent beings. Through them
she could see the white sails of the ship and the
rosy clouds in the sky. Their melodious voices
were so delicate that no human ear could hear
them, just as no human eye could see them. They
were so light that they floated in the air without
wings. And the little mermaid saw that she had a
body like theirs, and she felt herself rising higher
and higher above the foam.

"Where am I going?" she asked, and her voice
sounded like the others, so ethereal that no earthly
words can describe it.

"To the daughters of the air," they answered.
"A mermaid has no immortal soul, and can never
get one unless she wins the love of a human being.
Her eternal existence is in the hands of another. The
daughters of the air have no immortal souls either,
but through good deeds they can create them. We fly
to the hot lands where the pestilent air kills men, and
there we bring coolness. We fill the air with the scent
of flowers, and bring health and refreshment. When
we have striven to do good for three hundred years,
we are given an immortal soul and eternal happiness.
You, a poor little mermaid, have striven with all your
heart to do the same as we do. Through your suf-
ferings you have raised yourself to the realm of
the spirits of the air, and now, through good deeds,
you too can create an immortal soul for yourself."

The little mermaid stretched her transparent arms toward the sun, and for the first time, she shed tears.

On the ship she saw the prince and his beautiful bride looking for her. They stared sadly at the bubbling sea foam, as if they knew she had thrown herself into the waves. Unseen, she kissed the bride's forehead, smiled on the prince, then rose up with the other daughters of the air to the rosy cloud floating above. ❧